ERNEST'S GIFT

ERNEST'S GIFT

BY KATHRYN TUCKER WINDHAM

ILLUSTRATED BY FRANK HARDY

Junebug Books
Montgomery

PUBLISHED IN COOPERATION WITH THE
SELMA-DALLAS COUNTY PUBLIC LIBRARY

Junebug Books
P.O. Box 1588
Montgomery, AL 36102

Library of Congress Cataloging-in-Publication Data

ISBN 1-58838-149-8

Design by Randall Williams and Rhonda Reynolds

Printed in Korea by Pacifica Communications

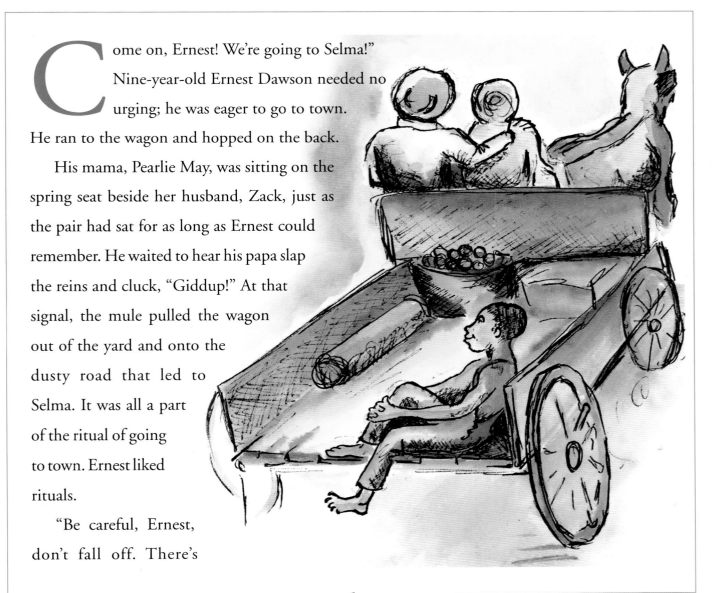

ome on, Ernest! We're going to Selma!"
Nine-year-old Ernest Dawson needed no
urging; he was eager to go to town.
He ran to the wagon and hopped on the back.

His mama, Pearlie May, was sitting on the
spring seat beside her husband, Zack, just as
the pair had sat for as long as Ernest could
remember. He waited to hear his papa slap
the reins and cluck, "Giddup!" At that
signal, the mule pulled the wagon
out of the yard and onto the
dusty road that led to
Selma. It was all a part
of the ritual of going
to town. Ernest liked
rituals.

"Be careful, Ernest,
don't fall off. There's

rough places in the road," his mama warned. That warning was part of the ritual, too.

As they picked up speed, one of the wagon wheels began to squeak. "Meant to grease that wheel before we left home," his papa said. "Wish you had," his mama replied. "That noise bothers me."

Ernest liked the sound of the squeaky wheel. It seemed to be singing to him, "Going to Selma. Going to Selma. Going to Selma." He tried to remember the first time he had been to town, but he couldn't. "I must have been a little baby," he decided, and he wondered what it was like to be held in his mama's arms all the way to town.

He remembered when he used to sit on a quilt, one his grandmother made, in the bed of the wagon. He was too little to see over the sides then. Now, riding backwards with his legs dangling and his bare feet nearly touching the road, he could see everything: the pine thickets, the cotton fields, the clusters of tenant houses, the creeks, an occasional church, cattle grazing in the pastures. Next year, 1932, he would be ten, old enough to drive the wagon. He had written the date on the wall beside his bed, a reminder of his papa's promise to let him hold the reins by himself then.

He was already old enough to wander around town by himself, didn't have to stay with his mama or his papa all the time. Sometimes he liked to sit quietly on the long bench where the men gathered outside the Yellow Front Store and listen to them talk. Today he wanted to explore.

"Watch the clock on the courthouse and be sure to be back here at the Yellow Front by twelve o'clock," his papa told him.

Ernest knew how to tell time. It was his job to wind the big clock on the shelf above the fireplace in the front room. Every now and then when he was winding the clock, using the brass key that hung on a nail by the hearth, his papa would say,

"Don't never let the clock run down. Time is important. Don't never be late." Ernest never was late, not ever in his whole life.

He could read well, too. He liked books, liked to read about places he had never been and about people who shaped history. He read his Bible every night, and he promised himself that when he was older he would read it all the way through from Genesis to Revelations.

He wished he had books to read about Indians. He picked up arrowheads, pocketfuls of them, when he followed behind his papa's plow. He wondered about the people who had shaped those arrowheads and had fashioned the pieces of pottery he sometimes found.

"When I get grown," Ernest used to say, "I'm going to have a room full of books in my house, books stacked all the way from the floor to the ceiling."

Like a magic carpet, his love of books may have drawn Ernest without his knowing it to the Carnegie Library that summer day in Selma. A library! Not just a room full of books but a whole building filled with them. Ernest had never been in a library. Nobody had ever told him there was a library in Selma, but there it stood, a big stone building with CARNEGIE LIBRARY carved over the doorway. He did not know what CARNEGIE meant, but he knew the word LIBRARY.

Ernest ran up the steps and pushed open
the heavy door. He entered a room like none
he had ever seen before. For a moment he was
transfixed, staring around in wonder.

Then a woman behind a tall counter
asked in a stern voice: "What do you
want, boy?" She glared at him over the
top of her glasses.

"I want to read some of those books,
please, ma'am." Ernest replied.

The woman glared harder, and her
voice had a brittle edge of contempt as
she spat out, "The books in this library
are for white people. We do not let
colored people read them. Please leave!"

Ernest turned quickly and stumbled
out the door. He did not want the
woman to see him cry.

The day was ruined. He walked slowly, not raising his head to look at anything, back to the Yellow Front Store. He took a place at the end of the bench long before noon. He tried, but he could not concentrate on the men's conversations. The hot dog his papa bought him was tasteless. He had to be reminded to thank his uncle for a stick of candy he did not even eat.

Later he almost choked on the frozen custard his Shannon cousins shared with him. He wondered if those cousins had ever tried to go to the library, but he did not ask.

Ernest wanted to go home. He was glad when the clock in the Presbyterian Church steeple struck four, glad to see his papa get up from the bench and give his friends a farewell hand-shake.

"Time to head home," his papa said. "Me and Ernest got to do some chores, and we got to get ready to go to church tomorrow. It's Choir Appreciation Day. You all come. There'll be lots to eat. Pearlie May will bring a coconut cake—if Ernest don't eat it before we get to church!"

The men laughed, and Ernest tried to smile at his papa's gentle teasing. He helped his parents put their purchases in the wagon, watched the mule take a long drink from the watering trough, and then climbed on the back of the wagon.

The wheel on the wagon still squeaked, but it no longer sang a happy song to Ernest. Now it seemed to say, "No books for colored. No books for colored. No books for colored."

They were nearly home when his papa turned to him and asked, "What's the matter, son?"

Ernest blurted out the whole ugly story. "Why, Papa? Why?" he sobbed. "Why can't I go in that library and read books? It's not fair!"

His papa did not answer immediately. Ernest thought perhaps he had not heard his question. Then, in a tone of voice he had never heard his papa use before, he said slowly, "No, son, it ain't fair. It ain't right. But that's the way things are, just the way things are. Maybe some day they'll change. Maybe. It'll take a miracle though."

His mama didn't say anything, but Ernest could hear her sniffling as though she might be crying.

The three of them never mentioned the library again.

Ernest tried to forget the harsh words, the hurt they caused. Going to Choir Appreciation Day at Isabella Baptist Church helped. He was proud when he heard people bragging on his mama's coconut cake, and he managed to grin when one of papa's friends thanked him for not eating it all up. All his life Ernest had gone to church with his parents. He did not always listen to the sermon his uncle preached, but he did sit quietly through the long service. Some Sundays he counted the planks in the walls of the building, and some Sundays he counted the knotholes. On summer Sundays he looked out the open windows at the cotton fields that almost encircled the church.

Dirt daubers and wasps often flew through the open windows and droned around the heads of worshippers. Ernest wanted to laugh when ladies began swatting at the flying insects with their pocketbooks and fans, but his papa frowned at him and shook his head.

One Sunday the preacher had to stop right in the middle of his sermon when a swarm of wasps began circling the pulpit. Members of the Board of Deacons and the Usher Board came to the rescue and shooed the intruders away. One of Ernest's aunts said the Devil sent those wasps. Ernest wasn't sure about that, and he forgot to ask his papa.

Occasionally the preacher talked about miracles. Ernest listened then. He tried to picture the parting of the Red Sea and the walls of Jericho falling down and Daniel in the lions' den. He liked to hear about the miracles Jesus did, too. The story of Jesus using a little boy's lunch to feed a great multitude of people may have been his favorite.

Ernest never lost his interest in the church. When he reached his teenage years, he sang in the choir and taught a Sunday School class, always in a position of leadership.

"Whatever Ernest did, he was always out front. He wasn't never no cow tail," one of his relatives said.

That ability for leadership carried over into other areas of his life. When he attended Knox Academy in Selma, he was a top scholar and president of his 1943 graduating class.

Knox Academy had a poor library, but there were books Ernest had not had access to before. He still could not go inside Selma's Carnegie Library. He still wondered why. After graduation, Ernest worked as a projectionist and helped manage the Roxy Theatre, a colored movie house on North Broad Street, until he entered the U.S. Navy in the late summer of 1943.

As was true for thousands of young men his age, military service in World War II changed Ernest's life. No longer was his world confined to Tyler and Selma. He went to places he had only read about, and, after his honorable discharge in 1946, he took advantage of the educational opportunities offered by the G.I. Bill.

First he graduated from the American Television Institute in Chicago. Then he moved to New York where, while working full time, he enrolled in night classes at City College, earning a B.S. Degree in mathematics. Somehow he found time to serve as a deacon in the Baptist Church (named Isabella like the church in Tyler) that an uncle established in Harlem. And he visited libraries.

Ernest tried teaching, but he became discouraged when teenagers in his classes showed little interest in learning. His students did not take advantage of the fine libraries open to them, and they stared at him in disbelief when he told them of his boyhood ejection from the Carnegie Library in Selma.

Friends suggested that he use his natural ability to entertain and instruct young children, his delight in reading and telling stories to little ones, and his God-given gentleness and patience to begin a new career in early childhood education. So Ernest enrolled again at City College to study for his degree in that field.

Ernest did love children, children of all races, and they returned his love. Co-workers observed that clusters of pre-schoolers followed him everywhere, clinging to him and listening to him and laughing. He liked to take his young charges, three and four and five years old, to libraries where they could handle the books, turn the pages and look at the bright pictures.

"Children need books," he used to say, "and so do their parents."

His appreciation of literature was combined with his enthusiasm for travel. Not only did he achieve his goal of visiting all fifty of the United States, he also traveled to nineteen foreign countries, making friends wherever he went. Always he took time to send cards to family members and friends back home and to collect pictures and books, even those in foreign languages, for his pupils.

Although he traveled worldwide, Ernest never forgot where he came from, never forgot the Tyler community and Selma. He made frequent visits home, and at the death of each parent (he had moved them to New York so he, an only child, could care for them) he accompanied their bodies back to Tyler for burial in the Isabella Baptist Church Cemetery.

On one of those trips home, he and a New York friend, Dr. Normal Paul, spent a morning in Selma. They were strolling along the downtown streets admiring the town's varied architecture, when their route took them by the public library.

"I suppose you spent a great deal of time here when you were growing up," Dr. Paul commented.

"No," Ernest replied. "No. You forget that I grew up in a segregated South. I was not allowed to go in the library."

Dr. Paul was silent. Then he chuckled. "Well, let's go in now," he said.

And they did.

The library staff welcomed them cordially, showed them around the building (new since Ernest's boyhood) and talked about plans for adding a children's wing to the facility. Ernest listened closely.

It took many months of planning and more months of raising money before construction on that children's wing started. Sometimes the committee handling the project became discouraged and almost gave up, but always a small miracle happened when spirits sank and the gloomy possibility of failure crept in.

One day many things had gone wrong, and spirits were especially low. Then came word that a prospective donor, a man the finance committee had counted on to make a large gift, had decided not to support the project.

"Maybe we aren't supposed to build this addition. Maybe those are signs that we should give up," a committee member moaned.

Just then a child, a mentally retarded child who found pleasure in visiting the library, came in with her mother. She walked over to the check-out desk and emptied her piggy bank. As the coins clattered on the counter, she said simply, "I brought my money to build God's library."

Faith never faltered again.

However, as the structure neared completion, the librarian became increasingly concerned about finding funds to stock the new shelves with books.

"What good is a wonderful new building if we can't buy books for the children? Where is the money coming from?" she wondered.

It was time for another miracle.

Then the letter arrived, the letter with the New York postmark. The letter said in part, "As executor of the estate of Ernest L. Dawson, I am writing to announce that Mr. Dawson has named the Selma Public Library as one of his beneficiaries. It would give me great pleasure to come to your library to present you with Ernest's donation of $10,000 in honor of his family."

Sometimes children, children of all races, in their reading room at the Selma Library, pause to look up on the wall at the photograph of a dark man with a gentle smile and laughing eyes. Most of the children are too young to read ERNEST DAWSON on the inscription under the picture, too young to understand that they are surrounded by a miracle of forgiveness and love.

The End